Maisie and the Botanic Garden Mystery

Author and illustrator Aileen Paterson

ROYAL BOTANIC GARDEN EDINBURGH

This book is dedicated to Lois Brown, Elspeth Scott, Joanna Fraser, David Lancry, Ethan Shanks and Teddy Thomson.

Thanks go to Lois Green and Janis Hogg for hints and tips, and to Val Bierman for the photograph of Louise's tree.

© Aileen Paterson

First Published in 2006 by
Royal Botanic Garden Edinburgh,
20a Inverleith Row,
Edinburgh, EH3 5LR, Scotland

E-mail: mailto:pps@rbge.ac.uk
URL: http://www.rbge.org.uk

ISBN 1 872291 35 X

Printed in Italy by Printer Trento S.r.l.

Reprint Code 10 9 8 7 6 5 4 3 2

Other Maisie titles in the Series:

Maisie and the
Botanic Garden Mystery

The Royal Botanic Garden Edinburgh, comprising of the Edinburgh Garden, Dawyck Botanic Garden, near Peebles, Benmore Botanic Garden, near Dunoon and Logan Botanic Garden, near Stranraer, is a world renowned centre of scientific and horticultural excellence, working at home and in more than 40 other countries globally with a mission to explore and explain the world of plants. It also flourishes as one of Scotland's most popular visitor attractions, welcoming over 700,000 people each year to its Edinburgh Garden alone.

Royal
Botanic Garden
Edinburgh

Maisie Mackenzie is a wee Scottish kitten who lives with her granny and daddy in Edinburgh. Their home is a flat in Morningside, next door to posh, pernickety, panloaf Mrs McKitty.

Cats in flats don't have gardens.

Maisie doesn't even have a sitooterie.

Maisie didn't know a daisy from a daffodil. She didn't know much about gardens at all, until one Wednesday last summer.

Everyone was busy that Wednesday morning. Granny was rushing off to catch the early train to the Highlands. Aunty Morag in Drumnadrookit had phoned to say she wasn't feeling very well. She'd had a touch of the

collywobbles (a very sore thing), so Granny wanted to go and cheer her up.

Maisie's daddy (a fearless explorer) was rushing too. He was going to a very important meeting, to talk about his travels in Togoland, Tobago and Lesmahagow.

But what about Maisie?

Who was looking after her?

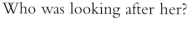

MRS McKITTY, that's who!

And Mrs McKitty was busy preparing a picnic.

She was taking Maisie and her friend Archie and her niece,
Lydia MacSporran of Lady Road, to The Botanic Garden.

Mrs McKitty was a dab hand at the baking. The kittens would

feast on salmon sandwiches, Melting Moments, cream sponge, and her famous pies --- the finest in Morningside! As soon as the picnic was packed and the kittens washed and brushed, they were off on the 23 bus. It went downhill all the way to the biggest garden in Edinburgh.

Maisie had never been to The Botanic Garden.

"Is it a good place for exploring and climbing trees?" she asked.

Mrs KcKitty gasped . . . "There will be No exploring and NO climbing trees, Maisie Mackenzie! You and Archie must not get up to any of your usual nonsense! Dear Lydia is going to paint some lovely flower pictures."

"I'm hungry," said Archie.

At last they arrived. They went through the big West Gate,
past the Botanics Shop, then walked down a long path to The
Woodland Garden. (Maisie was amazed to find that there were lots
of different gardens in The Garden.)

The Woodland Garden was lovely. Giant trees reached up to the

sky and the grass was soft under their paws. Mrs McKitty stopped
and put the picnic basket down.

"What a great place for adventures!" cried Maisie.

"What a great place for our picnic!" cried Archie.

But Mrs McKitty had other plans, and so did Lydia.

"Aunty Marjorie and I are going to look for a nice spot so I can do my paintings, aren't we, Aunty Marjorie?"

"Yes indeed," said Mrs McKitty. "Lydia will need peace and quiet to produce her best work. You two must stay here and keep an eye on the food until we return. Come along, Lydia."

Maisie and Archie didn't think much of that.

It wasn't long before they thought up a plan of their own. They decided to hide the basket in the middle of a clump of bushes. There was no one about. It would be hidden away and perfectly safe and they could go for a walk. Just a short one.

They followed a path which led them past a rocky garden
and crossed over a stream. They read the labels on the trees and
flowers and discovered that they came from all over the world.

Some had funny names. Maisie liked the Monkey Puzzle tree best. They met some ducks at the pond and some ladybirds marching over the grass. Then they got lost and went through a gate marked **PRIVATE** . . .

but they soon left
when they realised their
mistake! Luckily they found
a signpost which pointed the way
back to The Woodland Garden.

"I'll race you there", said Archie.

He ran ahead towards the giant trees and soon found the place where the picnic basket was hidden. He was pleased to see that there was no sign of Mrs McKitty and Lydia.

Maisie caught up with him just in time to hear him groan.
"What's the matter?" she asked "Are you alright?"

"No, I'm not alright. We're in terrible trouble. Mrs McKitty will go her dinger! Our hamper has scampered! Our goose is cooked! ! !"

"What GOOSE?" said Maisie "What are you talking about?"

"Come and look. The basket has vanished!"

It was a mystery. They hunted all over The Woodland Garden but it wasn't there.

Who could have taken it?

Where could it be?

"Come with me," said Maisie. "We need help."

"Where are we going?" asked Archie as they ran back along the path.

"I've no idea," said Maisie. "Let's start at the pond."

When they got there, the ducks weren't much help. They were too busy ducking and diving, but Maisie noticed that a strange visitor had joined them. The biggest bird she'd ever seen was standing in the water. He was a heron.

"Excuse me," she said, "I wonder if you can help us. I don't suppose you've seen a picnic basket anywhere? We've lost one."

The heron looked down his long beak at her.

"As a matter of fact, I have, just a few minutes ago when I was

flying over to the pond. It was
lying on the grass beside the
Glasshouse door."

The kittens thanked him and
hurried off.

They soon reached the
Glasshouse, but there was no sign
of the missing basket beside the
door. It had vanished AGAIN!

Archie began searching under the
trees while Maisie searched inside
the Glasshouse, just in case . . . It was
hot and sticky and steamy in there
and she found some daft-looking
plants but she didn't find what
she was looking for. She
was just about to leave
when she

heard meowing. It was coming from a pool filled with gigantic waterlilies. The leaves were as big as Granny's new rug! Maisie was amazed to see a tiny kitten sitting on one of the leaves!

"LOST!" meowed the kitten.

"Hello," said Maisie, "What's YOUR name?"

"Piccalilli. Lost. Time to go home. Eat Sausages."

Maisie laughed, but she realized the kitten was in danger.

It would be awful if she fell into the water. She must rescue her quickly.

Leaning out over the edge of the pool, Maisie managed to grab hold of the leaf. She tugged it towards her, then scooped up Piccalilli and carried her outside to safety.

Archie was waiting for her.

(Neither of them had found the basket.)

"Who's that?" he asked

"Her name is Piccalilli. She's lost. I found her inside.

This garden is full of surprises."

"You're right," said Archie "I've found something too. I was just standing here, minding my own business, when a crown fell out of

the sky! Look!"

"How peculiar," said Maisie, but Piccalilli smiled and reached out her paw. She took the little crown and put it on her head. It fitted perfectly.

"My hat!" she told them.

"MY HAT!" cried Maisie and Archie. "Is it really yours? Are you a princess?"

"Yes. Time to go home. I'm hungry."

"Me too," said Archie. "Come on, I'll give you a piggyback."

Now that Piccalilli was out of the big Glasshouse, she knew how to get home. She pointed to a path and said, "That way." They followed the path for what seemed a very long way, down a hill, past a little Chinese house and on into the farthest corner of The Garden. There behind some trees, another surprise awaited them . . .

A beautiful Queen Cat, wearing a flowery crown, sat in a bower
decorated with bright blue poppies.

"Home! Mama!" cried Piccalilli.

The Queen rose to greet them and thanked them for rescuing her little kitten. She told them that Piccalilli was always getting into pickles.

"I am Arabella," she said, "Queen of The Royal Botanic Garden. I look after it and all the cats who live here. My helpers searched everywhere for Princess Piccalilli, but all they found was a basket! It makes a comfy seat."

Maisie and Archie could hardly believe their eyes.

"That's our picnic basket! We've been looking everywhere for it."

"Then you must have it back, but I'm sorry to tell you that picnics are not allowed in my precious Garden. I like to keep it tidy."

"That's alright," said Archie. "We'll go to the park."

The Queen offered them some camomile tea. Maisie thanked her but said they had to go, because they were in a pickle too. They waved goodbye and ran all the way to The Woodland Garden.

When they arrived, Mrs McKitty and Lydia were waiting for them.

"Aunty Marjorie is very annoyed with you," said Lydia, helpfully.

Maisie and Archie both began to talk at once.

"We're very, very sorry. Have you been waiting for a long time?"

"Be quiet," thundered Mrs McKitty "I don't want to hear another word. Now tell me where you've been!"

The kittens were speechless, but Mrs McKitty was not.

"You are a disgrace to Morningside. Give me that basket at once. Lydia and I are starving."

"But you can't have picnics in The Botanic Garden," said Archie. "The Queen said so."

"The Queen?   What Queen?   Silence, Archibald! Lydia! – Open the basket."

The basket was opened.

Maisie and Archie gasped in horror! Lydia MacSporran's eyes popped and Mrs McKitty gave such a loud shriek that her hat blew off!

The basket was completely empty.

There were no salmon sandwiches, no Melting Moments, no cream sponge and not a single pie!

It was a mystery.

No one said a word. For once Mrs McKitty WAS speechless.

At last, she marched the kittens towards the Gate.

They were going home and when they got there, Maisie knew
she and Archie would have to explain everything. This would be
difficult. It was a long story and full of puzzles.

But she was about to get one more surprise . . .

Suddenly, she heard a familiar voice.

"Hello everyone! Hello Maisie! Imagine meeting you here."

It was Daddy! His very important meeting had been in The Botanic Garden. What a nice surprise!

"I'm just going to have lunch," he said. "Have you eaten yet?"

"No," said Archie.

"And whose fault is that?" said Mrs McKitty.

"Never mind," said Daddy. "Let me treat you all to lunch. There's a good café here, on the terrace."

So they all had lunch in The Garden.

And the lunch was SO delicious and Daddy said SUCH NICE THINGS about Lydia's paintings that Mrs McKitty quite forgot about the empty picnic basket!

BUT
THE
MYSTERY
REMAINS ...

WHO ATE ALL THE

WE DID!

MRS McKITTY'S
MELTING MOMENTS

Ingredients

125g/4oz butter or margarine

75g/3oz caster sugar

150g/5oz self-raising flour

Half an egg

Half teaspoonful almond essence
(optional)

Crushed cornflakes (enough to cover)

Equipment

1 Mixing Bowl

1 Baking Tray

Method

Cream the butter and sugar.

Beat in the egg and almond essence.

Mix in the flour.

Damp hands in water and roll small portions of the mixture into balls. Roll in crushed cornflakes.

Place the balls well apart on a greased baking tray and flatten each a little.

Bake for 10 – 15 minutes in a moderate oven… Gas Mark 5/190oC, until pale brown.

(Grown-up supervision required)

GLOSSARY

Go one's dinger	be very angry
Melting Moments	Small biscuits
Collywobbles	sore tummy
Pernickety	fussy
Panloaf	speaking with an affected accent
Sitooterie	a patio
Our goose is cooked	we are in big trouble
MY HAT	exclamation of surprise
A dab hand	very skilled